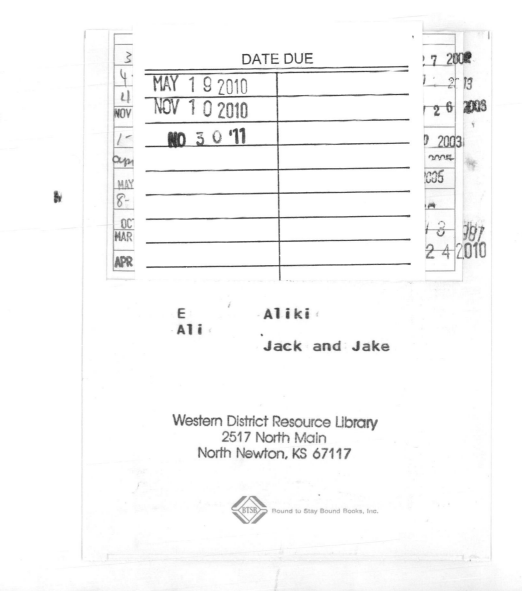

# JACK and JAKE

## ALIKI

Greenwillow Books  New York

Printed in Hong Kong by South China Printing Co.     First Edition     10 9 8 7 6 5 4 3 2 1

A black line was combined with watercolor paints for the full-color art. The text type is Korinna and the display type is Baskerville Flair.

For all the Jacks and Jakes

Library of Congress Cataloging in Publication Data     Aliki.     Jack and Jake.     Summary: A sister complains about the way everyone confuses her twin brothers. [1. Twins—Fiction. 2. Identity—Fiction. 3. Brothers and sisters—Fiction] I. Title.     PZ7.A397Jac 1986     [E]     85-9911     ISBN 0-688-06099-4 ISBN 0-688-06100-1 (lib. bdg.)

Why can't they tell Jack from Jake?

They said, "Jack is hungry," when it's Jake who cried.

They said, "Jake is wet," but it's Jack they dried.

They thought Jack was sleepy when Jake yawned and sighed.

What's wrong with them all?

They cooed over Jake when Jack learned how to crawl.

They said, "Jack's first tooth," when Jake started to bawl.

They shouted, "Catch Jake!" when they thought Jack would fall.

Why can't they get them straight?

Jack took his first steps. They said, "Jake can walk."

Jake cried out, "Bow-wow." They said, "Jack can talk."

And guess who they blamed when Jack broke the chalk?

The wrong one, of course.

Jack built a high tower. "Great, Jake," they all said.

Jake wanted more ice cream. Jack got it instead.

Jack sneezed and they cried out, "Put Jake into bed!"

Can't they see?

Jack tried and Jake tried to make them aware.

Jake gave himself freckles. Jack parted his hair.

But poor Jack and poor Jake—they still mixed the pair.

Why don't they look?

Why can't they learn? It's the same old mistake.

It's "Hi, Jake" to Jack and "Goodbye, Jack" to Jake.

"Which one," they whisper, "fell into the lake?"

That did it. I finally told them.

Jack does things and says things that only Jack could.

Jake finds things and likes things that only Jake would.

Jack's Jack and Jake's Jake—is that understood?

It's as simple as that.